New Tracks for Thomas

Based on *The Railway Series* by the Rev. W. Awdry

A Random House PICTUREBACK® • Illustrated by Owain Bell

Random House New York

Thomas the Tank Engine & Friends A BRITT ALLCROFT COMPANY PRODUCTION Based on The Railway Series by the Rev W Awdry. Copyright © Gullane (Thomas) LLC 1994. All rights reserved under International and Pan-American Copyright Conventions. Published in the United States by Random House, Inc., New York, and simultaneously in Canada by Random House of Canada Limited, Toronto. www.randomhouse.com/kids   www.thomasthetankengine.com
RANDOM HOUSE and colophon are registered trademarks of Random House, Inc.
Library of Congress Catalog Card Number: 93-85588   ISBN 0-679-85699-4
Printed in the United States of America   20 19 18 17 16 15

Early one morning, Sir Topham Hatt came to the train yard.

"Good morning, Thomas," he said. "I have big news! We are adding a passenger train to one of the freight branch lines. Because you have been doing such a good job, we want you to pull the new train once a day."

A new train! Thomas felt proud. There would be new tracks to ride on, a new platform to stop at, and a new station house to see. All for Thomas!

"Of course, there will be more passengers," said Sir Topham Hatt. "And more work."

"Oh, do not worry," Thomas told him in a boastful way. "I can do it. It will be easy!"

The other engines weren't so sure.

"You must go slowly at first," Edward said. "You must listen to your driver and be careful not to get lost."

Thomas was too excited to pay attention to old Edward. *He* might have trouble with new tracks, Thomas thought. But not me! I am a Really Useful Engine. That's why *I* am getting another station!

The new passenger train was to start running the very next day. "This is an important event," Sir Topham Hatt told everyone. "People will be coming from miles around!"

Thomas wanted to look his best. So that afternoon he was carefully washed down. Then he got a bright paint job. "Now I look shiny and new!" he said to Edward. "I look just the way a Really Useful Engine should!"

The next day, when Thomas's paint was quite dry, his coaches, Annie and Clarabel, got into place. The driver climbed into the cab, and they were off! *Clackety, clack.* Thomas was heading for the new station.

"Make sure you read the signs along the tracks," Sir Topham called to him. "Remember, Thomas! It is a new way for you to go."

NEW STATION

Edward shouted after Thomas, too. "Be careful!"
he said. "You don't want to lose your way."

But Thomas wasn't listening. "Peep, peep!"
he said as he chugged along. "I know what to do.
I know what to do!"

Soon Thomas picked up speed. *Clackety, clack.*
Clackety, clack.

"Slow down," said his driver. "We have to be
sure we are going the right way."

But Thomas only went quicker. He did not listen
to Sir Topham Hatt. He did not listen to Edward.
And he was not going to listen to his driver, either.
"Peep, peep! I know where to go," he said. "I know
where to go."

Now Thomas was going even faster. He whizzed past houses. He sped past farms and lakes.

Clackety, clack. Clackety, clack. Signs went by in a flash. "Slow down!" his driver said again. "We must read the signs!"

But Thomas didn't stop to read them. He wanted to get to the station as fast as he could. He wanted everyone to know he was a Really Useful Engine.

Soon Thomas grew tired. He slowed down just a bit and looked all around the countryside. He saw a water tower and cows grazing in a meadow, but they didn't look familiar. "Oh, my!" said Thomas. "Where am I?

"I didn't listen to Sir Topham Hatt, Edward, *or* my driver. I didn't even read the signs! I wasn't careful at all."

Claaaaackety, claaaaack. Claaaaaackety, claaaaaack. Thomas came to a stop. He felt just awful. Sir Topham Hatt was waiting for him at the new railroad station with all the new passengers. And where was Thomas?

Lost!

"Maybe I am not a Really Useful Engine after all," Thomas said sadly.

A big tear rolled down his cheek. Then Thomas sighed, and a puff of smoke billowed out his smokestack.

"Is that you, Thomas?" cried a voice in the distance. It was Sir Topham Hatt, coming around the bend! "I saw your smoke! Now move along. Everything is ready!"

"Peep, peep!" said Thomas. The railroad station was just down the track! Thomas started up once more.

How silly I am, thought Thomas. Of course nothing looks familiar. I have never been here before! If only I had read the signs. Then I would have known I was going the right way all along.

And Thomas hurried along the tracks, *clackety, clack*.

"Hooray, hooray!" the passengers shouted when they saw Thomas. Flags waved in the air, and a band began to play.

Sir Topham Hatt said, "Everybody on board! All aboard Thomas!"

Thomas smiled. He was at the new railroad station—and just in time! But then Thomas looked at his driver. He looked at Sir Topham Hatt. They did not look pleased. And Thomas knew something still wasn't right.

"I am sorry," he said to both of them. "I should have listened. I should have been more careful. Then I would have known I wasn't lost. I would have known I was going the right way all along."

Back at the train yard, Thomas said the same
thing to Edward. "I should have listened to you,"
he told his friend. "I should not have gone so
quickly."

Now Thomas was happy. He knew next time
he'd do it right. Next time he'd be a Really Useful
Engine.

And sure enough, Thomas was! *Clackety, clack.*
Clackety, clack. The following day, Thomas puffed
carefully along the new tracks and headed straight
to his new station!